Stop Mom

JENNA KAY

Storyshares

Published by Storyshares, LLC.

Storyshares
Storyshares, LLC
24 N. Bryn Mawr Avenue #340
Bryn Mawr, PA 19010-3304

www.storyshares.org

Aligned with the Science of Reading.

Interest Level: Ages 12+

ISBN 9798885974707

Book design by Storyshares

Storyshares

 **Storyshares**

GETTING STARTED

 These passages provide practice reading engaging and accessible connected text while supporting foundational literacy skills!

PRE-READING

- Review **phonics rules** that will help you decode the passage.
- **Preview** the text for examples of words that follow the rule(s).
- **Explore challenge words**. These are words the don't fit the decoding pattern.

WHILE READING

- **Read** as much as you can.
- Scoop the text into **meaningful phrases**.

AFTER READING

- **Summarize** the story.
- **Discuss** how you felt after reading. Was this a successful reading experience? Why or why not?
- Make a **prediction** for what will happen next.

SCOPE AND SEQUENCE

At Storyshares, we teach all six syllable types, in order of frequency in the English language, beginning with closed syllables, which account for just under 50 percent of English. This approach empowers students to read more, faster.

Consonant -le

R-Controlled Vowels

Vowel Teams

Vowel-Consonant-e

Schwa & Exceptions

Open Syllables

2+ Closed Syllables

Closed Syllables

These passages are cumulatively decodable, meaning that the passages include words that help students practice phonics concepts that were taught earlier in the scope and sequence.

⭐ **Skills covered in this set**

"Stop Mom"

/ o / sound

short "o"

Bob	fog	lot	slob
bond	got	mom	snot
boss	hog	mop(ped)	spot
clock	hop	not	stomped
cop	hot	on	stop(ped)
cross	lost	shock	top

challenge words

coffee	looked	smiled
forgot	morning	thanks
heels	ohhh	ugh

high-frequency regular words

am	game	live	room
but	like	now	up

high-frequency irregular words

do	into	talk
have	love	what

"Bob. BOB!"

It was my mom.

I did not talk.

"BOB," said mom.

She stomped into my room.

"What, Mom?"

Mom looked cross.

She was not sad.

100% mad.

"You are a slob, Bob!" Mom said.

Ugh. I do not live like a hog.

I said, "Stop, Mom!"

Mom was mad.

But I am not a slob.

Now I am mad.

I am not that bad.

Mom said, "Grab a mop."

I did not talk.

"Hop to it!" Mom snapped.

I got up. "Ugh, Mom."

I got the mop.

Mom was hot on my heels.

"Not like that," Mom said, "you missed a spot."

"Stop, Mom!"

Mom stopped.

I mopped and mopped with the mop.

Mom was still on top of me. Like she is the boss. Like she is a cop.

I stopped. I looked at the clock.

Ohhh.

I forgot.

Morning mom is NOT on top of her game.

I forgot. But I got this...

"Hot coffee, Mom?"

Mom stopped.

She was in shock.

She smiled.

"Thanks, Bob," Mom said.

"You are a snot. But I love you a lot."

"You are not my boss," I said. "But I love you a lot."

We have a bond that is not lost in the morning fog.

About the Author

Jenna Kay is a fiction writer who brings warmth and curiosity to every story she creates. Known for her keen eye for character and sharp sense of voice, she transforms everyday moments into narratives that resonate with readers of all ages. When she isn't writing, Jenna enjoys exploring local coffee shops, tending to her ever-growing collection of houseplants, and discovering new trails to hike.

About The Publisher

Storyshares is focused on supporting the millions of teens and adults who struggle with reading by creating a new shelf in the library specifically for them. The ever-growing collection features content that is compelling and culturally relevant for teens and adults, yet still readable at a range of lower reading levels.

Storyshares generates content by engaging deeply with writers, bringing together a community to create this new kind of book. With more intriguing and approachable stories to choose from, the teens and adults who have fallen behind are improving their skills and beginning to discover the joy of reading. For more information, visit storyshares.org.

Easy to Read. Hard to Put Down.

Scan to learn more and browse our collections

Thank you for using Storyshares, your Pathway to Literacy for striving readers in grades 3+.

Please keep in touch. We have...

- **Free Resources**
- **Intervention Curriculum for grades 6-12**
- **Decodable Chapter Book series for upper elementary, middle school, and high school**
- **A digital library with 500+ high-low and decodable titles**
- **Professional development for educators**

Follow Us

 @storyshares

 /StorysharesLiteracy

 @storyshares

 /company/story-shares

Continue the conversation!

www.storyshares.org

info@storyshares.org